Fictional Fun

THE SOUTH

EDITED BY DONNA SAMWORTH

First published in Great Britain in 2011 by:

Remus House
Coltsfoot Drive
Peterborough
PE2 9BF
Telephone: 01733 890066
Website: www.youngwriters.co.uk

Book Design by Ali Smith & Spencer Hart

SB ISBN 978-0-85739-414-9

FOREWORD

Young Writers was established in 1990 with the aim of encouraging and nurturing writing skills in young people and giving them the opportunity to see their work in print. By helping them to become more confident and expand their creative skills, we hope our young writers will be encouraged to keep writing as they grow.

School pupils nationwide have been exercising their minds to create their very own short stories, Mini Sagas, using no more than fifty words, to be included here in our latest competition, *The Adventure Starts Here ...*

The entries we received showed an impressive level of creativity and imagination, providing an absorbing look into the eager minds of our future authors.

YE CONTENTS OF AUTHORS

Congratulations to all young writers who appear in this book

Finlay Community School, Gloucester

St James the Great RC Primary School, Thornton Heath

St Joseph's Catholic Primary School, Chalfont St Peter

St Joseph's Catholic Primary School, Haywards Heath

Soho Parish School, London

Someries Junior School, Luton

Winslow CE Combined School, Winslow

MINI SAGAS

JACK AND THE BEANS

Unexpectedly Ben came back to his huge house. His mum sent him to his room for getting beans instead of money. He threw them out of the window, into a deep hole.
The next day the beans had grown into a sugar stalk. Ben ate it all up and ... *bang!*

Thomas Goodchild (9)
Aylesbury Vale Pupil Referral Unit, Aylesbury

BENEDICT AND THE ALIEN

Unexpectedly when Benedict was playing football he heard a bang. It was piercing, then it went silent. A massive UFO landed with an enormous *boom!* The glistening door opened, the fiendish alien took Benedict inside. In a flash it disappeared into the sky.
Would Benedict ever be found again ... ?

Benedict Marlow (10)
Aylesbury Vale Pupil Referral Unit, Aylesbury

MYTHS AND LEGENDS

Slowly, massive snow-capped mountains loomed into sight through the misty moors. Dark shadowy outlines of a multitude of people appeared. Suddenly, a pack of salivating wolves ambushed them. The mob turned and sprinted like cheetahs. The wolves followed in hot pursuit. Mysteriously, a magical muscular beast saved the day.

Tristan Dixon (11)

Aylesbury Vale Pupil Referral Unit, Aylesbury

GALAXAR AND THE PRINCESS OF THE BAT AND TACKLE SHOP

Once lived a very evil wizard, his name was Galaxar. Galaxar's enemy was Princess Tiana. Tiana's dad was king of the bat and tackle shop so that made Tiana a princess.

Once her dad took her swimming. Whilst in the pool, she mysteriously disappeared but Galaxar got away with it.

Anya Wheatley (8)

Bishop Road Primary School, Bishopston

HAUNTED!

'Don't go inside!' Those were the last words Mary ever pleaded to Jessie. No one knew what made her go. The only evidence of her having been there was her battered satchel lying at the steps of the house.
What made her do it? Everyone knew the house was haunted.

Jessica Reynolds (8)

Bishop Road Primary School, Bishopston

THE CAPTURED MERMAID

The mermaid sat on the deserted rock. The pirates had tied her up.
Meanwhile Old Donkey was watching from the shore. He called his friend Dolphin, threw him his false teeth and told him what to do. Dolphin bit through the rope with Donkey's false teeth. The mermaid was free.

Maddie McDermott (8)

Bishop Road Primary School, Bishopston

THE LILY POND

Mary hated camping. When she was getting water she saw a lily pond. She looked down and suddenly she was sucked in; there was silence.
The next thing she knew she was in the middle of the ocean surrounded by mermaids. She looked down and found she had a tail.

Rosie Hardiman (9)
Bishop Road Primary School, Bishopston

MANOR HOUSE MYSTERIES

It had been a day at the manor house, and since then nothing felt right to Emily. You see, Emily had had this dream of a ghost - Edward. When she woke, she was relieved but something struck, something creepy. She was right, something was waiting alright, just around the corner ...

Helena Rogowski (8)
Bishop Road Primary School, Bishopston

GHOSTLY SCARES

He heard a scream, at the point of the clock tower. He stumbled up the ladder in disbelief. There it was again, another scream. Then suddenly an object came falling down. *Bang!* It slammed straight into the concrete, but there was nothing there, it had disappeared.

Jonathan Corrigan (9)

Burgoyne Middle School, Potton

THE JUMP!

I was walking down the road, through the park and into the wood. There are many myths about this wood, but I was just walking home from school.
I heard some rustling but I wasn't scared, I walked down there every day.
Suddenly, a giant bear came out! I jumped.

Thomas Smart (10)

Burgoyne Middle School, Potton

THE MERMAID AND THE KNIGHT

Once upon a time, a mermaid found a statue of a knight so she took it to the eagle-headed lion monkey, and hocus-pocus, it turned into a real knight! They got married, had children and the whole process started again!

Michael Tennant (9)
Burgoyne Middle School, Potton

HANG IN THERE!

The road was long and dirty. The wind howled and Tom shivered. His foot slipped on the wet surface. He saw a huge, horrible house. He went in. There were gaping jaws in front of him. A man in front spoke. 'Now Tom. Time for your dental appointment. Sit down!'

Gareth Thomas (12)
Burgoyne Middle School, Potton

THE ROLLER COASTER

Selena stepped onto the dusty cart. She stopped and sighed. Did she want to get on? Yes! She sat on the tattered seat, there was a slight creak and she was off! Suddenly a crash echoed around the tunnel and the wheel came off! Selena fell into a black hole.

Christina Anker (9)

Burgoyne Middle School, Potton

HISSOUT

Tom was going to bed after a long trip. He closed the door and he did his usual check behind the door. After that he went to bed.

He heard a hissing sound. His heart pumped out of him, but to his relief his dad was making the hissing sound.

Ainanshe Ali (12)

Burgoyne Middle School, Potton

SNOW WHITE AND THE SEVEN DWARFS

Snow White ran into a small cottage and to her surprise seven pairs of red eyes were glaring at Snowy out of the gloom. 'I kill you!' screamed seven dwarfs from the dark gloom and started chasing Snowy around the house.
Snowy got scared. She ran all the way home.

Joshua Warner (9)

Burgoyne Middle School, Potton

VAMPIRE EGGS

There was something in the wardrobe going *blur, blur,* so he opened it with a shock. It was a vampire covered in eggs. He screamed and ran to his parents. They told him to go back to bed. He went.
Next morning, his parents found him covered in blood.

Joe Gauge (9)

Burgoyne Middle School, Potton

THE THREE LITTLE PIGS

Three pigs built houses made of straw, wood and brick. Two of them were dead because a wolf ate them after blowing their houses down. The third was safe in his strong brick house; and when the wolf climbed down the chimney, he fell into a pot of boiling water!

Rosie Robinson (9)

Bute House Preparatory School, Hammersmith

A MIDNIGHT MISSION

The still night was disturbed by the creaking of the thin slippery branch beneath me. Finally I'd reached the summit of this majestic, graceful oak. Amazement dwindled rapidly into fear. The path below was no longer visible. Starting to feel queasy I called out desperately, hoping I'd be heard, *'Miaow!'*

Rasnika Wasan (9)

Bute House Preparatory School, Hammersmith

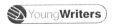

SHIVERING SEARCH

'Poppy!' Isabella bellowed, exhaustedly.
Glistening, swirling snowflakes falling thickly through the skeleton-like trees hid Poppy's footprints. Abruptly, the storm ceased, revealing delicate paw prints and a whimpering plea. Hurriedly, she tracked the trail, tracing Poppy's path. Tangled in the brambles stood a bedraggled Poppy, shivering but found at last.

Imogen Culhane (9)

Bute House Preparatory School, Hammersmith

THE INTRUDER AT MIDNIGHT

Thump! Charlotte awoke startled!
As she tiptoed down the stairs she thought a spine-chilling thought, *is it an intruder?*
Finally she reached the bottom of the stairs and gasped, 'Midnight!'
As Midnight stepped out of the fireplace, Charlotte picked him up and hugged her small, sooty cat in relief.

Maddie Lloyd (9)

Bute House Preparatory School, Hammersmith

REVENGE

'History test!' announced the teacher cheerfully. I groaned; history was my worst subject and now Gemma would laugh at me. I tried my best but it was just horrible. Test results now, the top mark was ... 'Katy Robinson.' Me? At last I had got my revenge on Gemma. Gemma sulked.

Victoire Guéroult (9)

Bute House Preparatory School, Hammersmith

HOMECOMING

Exploding bombs dropping everywhere, wartime was no fun for the boisterous brothers, Conor and Euan. Having spent their third night in the damp, noisy shelter, they wearily meandered home.
Eyes tired and blinded by the morning sun, a familiar silhouette was on their doorstep. Hearts racing, Dad was home!

Madeleine Symes (9)

Bute House Preparatory School, Hammersmith

THE SHADOW

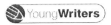

She couldn't sleep. Moonlight trickled through the shutters, casting shadows across the carpet. Owls hooted eerily outside. Something wasn't quite right.
The door creaked. Uneasily, Tess sat up. A sleek, sinister silhouette glided into the room. Terrified, she slid under the duvet, heart pounding. Then she realised. 'Get off Puss!'

Sasha Harden (10)
Bute House Preparatory School, Hammersmith

CHRISTMAS DAY

As I sat on the edge of my bed waiting for reindeer bells, the doorbell suddenly rang. On the doorstep stood an old man dressed in red. 'Can I use your loo please?'
Stunned, I pointed the way.
'Thank you, Merry Christmas,' he shouted, jumping into his sleigh, whooshing away.

Natasha Wheatland (9)
Bute House Preparatory School, Hammersmith

CHRISTMAS SURPRISE!

I stood in fright. I was positive Father Christmas would have delivered his presents. What if he had forgotten? Suddenly, a muffled bell rang. I crept to see if anything was there. My eyes felt like they would burst! In the middle of the piano, stacked randomly, were my presents!

Pandora Mackenzie (9)

Bute House Preparatory School, Hammersmith

A PAINFUL LESSON

Sitting in the hospital whilst the doctor glued my forehead, I was feeling both scared and silly. It seemed like harmless fun when we started playing gypsies at home. Fleeing down the stairs, I'd stumbled and landed, head against a wooden statue. I'd felt something warm running down my face.

Annie Roberts (9)

Bute House Preparatory School, Hammersmith

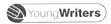

SUSPENSE ON SAFARI

I was walking along the tranquil riverbank. The only sound was the soft buzzing of bees and the distant chirping of birds. Suddenly, I heard a commotion. I never should have left the safety of the safari camp! I slowly turned to see an innocent little bird. What a relief!

Ella Scott (10)
Bute House Preparatory School, Hammersmith

SNOOPY SUSIE

Susie was playing when she noticed the house. The local villagers said it was haunted. She crept cautiously into the deserted house. As Susie stepped forward, a pale figure in a white sheet swooped at her. She screamed and ran to the door. She learnt not to snoop around again.

Noor Sawhney (10)
Bute House Preparatory School, Hammersmith

A SHOCK!

The sea lapped at Daisy's feet. She dived in. Daisy felt something nibble her toes - to her horror a shark's fin appeared! Frightened, she swam to shore, the shark close behind! Clambering onto the beach, she turned - instead of a shark her brother stood with his shark fin hat, laughing!

Uma Baron (9)

Bute House Preparatory School, Hammersmith

ROBOTIC NIGHTMARE

I could hear the pounding footsteps of the robot behind me. Laser beams stopped me from escaping. I flinched at the screeching of the nanobots coming from both sides. I was trapped. My stomach churned as the robot launched me upwards. I was falling - 'Jake, get off the computer, now!'

Nicole Borgers (10)

Bute House Preparatory School, Hammersmith

AM I LOST?

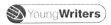

I turned around. My mother was nowhere to be seen. I began to feel uneasy. There were so many people I could barely see anything. I ran as fast as possible to the mall's service desk. My heart was racing. I turned around and there she was. Reunited at last.

Alessandra Waggoner (9)

Bute House Preparatory School, Hammersmith

DID IT MOVE?

The room was empty apart from a large box. Did it move? She wasn't sure. Sophie nervously tiptoed over. As she got closer, she began to hear snuffling, scuffling noises. Gingerly, she opened the box. Out scampered a tiny furry ball. A puppy!
'Happy birthday, dear!'

Anna Carse (9)

Bute House Preparatory School, Hammersmith

HAUNTED!

Stopping as she heard a blood-curdling scream, Amy turned around finding no one. A cackle came from the darkness, suddenly a creature swooped down and grabbed her feet. She was terrified ...
She woke up, her heart racing, a dream never to be had again!

Anjali Pillai (9)

Bute House Preparatory School, Hammersmith

THE GIFT OF HOPE

Flashy, noisy, slick, plastic. Hope wanted none of it. All she wanted for Christmas was snow. With worried brows and wringing hands, her parents lamented they'd stay in temperate Texas this holiday.
After Midnight Mass, the towering church doors were flung open, revealing flittering little miracles.
'Snow!' Hope rejoiced.

Sophie Dawson (10)

Bute House Preparatory School, Hammersmith

THE ART COMPETITION

Jenny came home from school, she hadn't had a very nice day. A blanket of snow carpeted the ground, yet she wasn't allowed out at break. She put on her coat and opened the door. Just then, the phone rang.
'Hello?' she said.
'You've won the art competition!' someone answered.

Kay Hanson (9)
Bute House Preparatory School, Hammersmith

A RESTLESS NIGHT

Midnight, 1am, I couldn't sleep. It seemed seconds later when my alarm rang. Feeling black and blue, I checked under the mattress. Nothing! I trudged to breakfast. My teddy was on the table. 'Princess, found you!' Lifting her, I spotted something which had rolled there during supper: a tiny pea!

Ismay Forsyth (10)
Bute House Preparatory School, Hammersmith

LOST - ALISON

One Sunday James, Alison and I went to church with Gran and on the way home called at the supermarket.
Five minutes later Alison was missing and her name and description were announced over the loudspeaker system.
Alison was found in the bakery enjoying herself and we returned home.

Isabel Roberts (9)

Bute House Preparatory School, Hammersmith

CHASED

My friends and I were going on a picnic in the vineyards. Suddenly, we heard scuffing and rustling nearby. *A wild boar!* I thought.
We turned and ran to the house but then we looked back and saw the farmer's floppy-eared puppy chasing us! He just wanted to play.

Abigail Adebiyi (9)

Bute House Preparatory School, Hammersmith

CHOOSE!

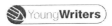

'Choose!' Katy's mum urged impatiently.
Katy stared hopelessly at the tiny fur balls with melting brown eyes. How could she choose one?
Suddenly, a fluffy puppy leapt onto her lap and soaked her face with puppy slobber. 'He is the one!' Katy screamed joyfully, and they were best friends forever!

Alexandra Riklin (9)
Bute House Preparatory School, Hammersmith

SURPRISE

Katrina walked down the garden path, humming happily. The sun was shining, and the sky was blue. Nothing would stop today being a good day. Katrina heard a rustle in the bushes, not far from her. She jumped suddenly. She got closer. 'Argh!' Katrina screamed.
'Boo! Got you scaredy-cat!'

Juliette Giscard d'Estaing (9)
Bute House Preparatory School, Hammersmith

CRASH-LANDING!

I had a feeling the end was near. The engines whirred. The clocks changed across the Prime Meridian, then a sudden jerk, down, down, down. It felt like we were plunging into the centre of the Earth. Crash-landing! Almost! Then everything abruptly stopped. Flight - AA 1043 had landed safely!

Romy Caton-Jones (9)

Bute House Preparatory School, Hammersmith

IT'S NOT FAIR!

I arrived home from school and silence haunted the hallway. I walked into the living room to find my know-it-all elder brother sitting on the sofa watching TV, looking sorry for himself. At this I started to fill up with jealousy. *'It's not fair!'*

Susannah Phillips (9)

Bute House Preparatory School, Hammersmith

AMELIA-ANNE

I was playing on the beach with my new friend, Amelia-Anne. She didn't want to swim so we made sandcastles instead.
When I got home I told Grandma about the girl in the long pinafore.
'Amelia-Anne drowned in 1914, more than fifty years ago!' she told me softly.

Ruby Blackwood (9)
Bute House Preparatory School, Hammersmith

CRYING

Rebecca silently screamed at the man who had dared come here. He stood uneasily in the corner. Tears flowed down Rebecca's cheeks when she saw what he had become. Choking back her tears she asked, 'How could you do this?'
'Cut! Great, great job, darling, you really can act!'

Matilda Ford (9)
Bute House Preparatory School, Hammersmith

THE KOOIKERHONDJE

Mike had always wished he could have a puppy. A cute, sweet Kooikerhondje.
One day, he was walking home when a Kooikerhondje ran towards him. It licked Mike's face. Mike looked at the name tag. His home address was on it! He sprinted home with the puppy ... 'Surprise!'

Emily de Vegvar (10)

Bute House Preparatory School, Hammersmith

DON'T DOUBT SANTA

Alex was distraught when I broke the news. We were going to Gran's for Christmas. We had no electricity. It was Christmas Eve, 'Santa will never find us.'
We woke early, was there any point searching for presets? There were loads! We should not have doubted Santa, he always knows.

Sophie Carroll (9)

Bute House Preparatory School, Hammersmith

A NOISE AT MIDNIGHT

It was pitch-black when I walked out of my cosy bedroom at midnight. Then I heard a creak from behind me. I did a sudden turn to look, but no one was there. I then heard an extremely loud bark. It was only my beloved black and white dog.

Katherine Chulack (9)

Bute House Preparatory School, Hammersmith

MONSTER MADNESS

One day Jason's mother reminded him some friends were coming. He should Hoover the lounge. He opened the cupboard door. A monster sprang out and said, 'You'd be nice on toast!' in a familiar voice.
Was it Pete? 'It must be him. I locked him in there an hour ago!'

Amy Stocks (9)

Bute House Preparatory School, Hammersmith

MYSTERIOUS

It was dark and gloomy and it didn't help that I was lost in a spooky forest. I walked on but I could still feel breathing behind me. I turned around. No one was there. Then I fell. I gulped. I turned slowly. There was a … oh, only a badger!

Samantha Flint (9)

Bute House Preparatory School, Hammersmith

OOPS!

Billy, the cat's owner, had shut him out again. He knocked on the door of his house. Two dogs walking past stared in amazement. An unfamiliar woman opened the door. Seeing nobody she shut it. Billy knocked again, but this time sprang at her. 'The next-door neighbour's cat!' Oops!

Helena Walford (9)

Bute House Preparatory School, Hammersmith

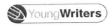

CHRISTMAS EVE

I looked up to find sixteen black legs galloping across the midnight sky. There was complete silence, slowly people started to disappear into their houses. My heart was thumping against my chest. I was terrified ...
'Ho, ho, ho, it's Santa's sledge.'

Ava Lottig (9)
Bute House Preparatory School, Hammersmith

FALSE ALARM!

I walked reluctantly into a dimly lit room and a leering man with thin, evil-looking eyes advanced menacingly, brandishing a sharp needle. I squeezed my eyes shut tight in fear. Suddenly, I heard my mother's warm, gentle voice saying, 'Don't worry, it's only an injection!'
What a great relief!

Consuelo Monson (10)
Bute House Preparatory School, Hammersmith

THE EVIL MASTER

Louise always obeyed her evil master. One day, he told her to build a rocket. She gathered all her friends and asked them for help. They put together their ideas and soon had a rocket. The evil master jumped in, flew up to space and never returned.

Isabel Harley (9)

Bute House Preparatory School, Hammersmith

MYSTERY VAMPIRE

Rat-a-tat-tat! Jenny looked through the window. A menacing figure stood outside, waiting. He looked like a vampire and Jenny was shaken, frightened and scared. She opened the door and heard a, 'Trick or treat?'
'Of course,' Jenny cried, 'it's Halloween!'

Libby Bryant (9)

Bute House Preparatory School, Hammersmith

NIGHTMARE

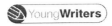

Grotesque beasts, gargoyles everywhere making Lily's heart skip a beat. Rustling trees winding around Lily, screaming uneven sequences; pitch-black darkness, with nowhere to run for safety. *Tick-tock* goes Lily's future until *bang!*
'Lily!' called her meek little mother. 'Are you OK?'
'Dreaming,' Lily replied in the deepest relief.

Charlotte Parry (9)
Bute House Preparatory School, Hammersmith

ANYONE THERE?

Lea woke up and got ready for school. 'Don't worry, Mum, I'll walk,' she said.
She reached school, it looked deserted! Looking up at the school clock she realised that the clocks had gone back last night. 'Not an hour of waiting,' she groaned, slumping against the railings unhappily.

Shikha Yadav (9)
Bute House Preparatory School, Hammersmith

LONDON DUNGEON

The room went pitch-black. I was sitting on the end, so the figure came up to me. He pulled away his cloak and was about to stab me!
I told my friends the story and they said they didn't see the figure but I did - in the London Dungeons.

Lara Defries (9)

Bute House Preparatory School, Hammersmith

TRUMPET, MY HERO

My pet elephant, Trumpet and I rode down to the beach near our farm in Africa. I was puzzled as the ocean vanished beneath our feet. We had less than a minute to escape when the titanic tsunami wave came thrashing into the shore. Trumpet saved my life that day.

Lucetta Edward (9)

Bute House Preparatory School, Hammersmith

GAME OVER

I'm running faster and faster down a dark alley. A man follows me. He has a gun. I skid and fall. The man gets closer still. Then I reach a dead end. The man lifts his gun and shoots. I fall. *Game Over* flashes across my computer screen.

Annabel Quick (10)
Bute House Preparatory School, Hammersmith

THE CREAK IN THE HALLWAY

Everyone was fast asleep. I was just about to reach for the lamp when I heard a creak. I grabbed my robe and flung it over my shoulders as I crept towards the door. The door burst open. I turned on the light. 'Do you like chocolate?' asked the Easter Bunny.

Iona Fairhead (10)
Bute House Preparatory School, Hammersmith

THE PIED GUITARIST OF TOKYO

In downtown Tokyo a punk sat scoffing sushi. The newspaper read: 'Pompous people in Tokyo. Reward for anyone to drive them away'. He took his guitar and stood up to the challenge. Loudly he played rock and with fingers in ears, pompous people were never to be seen again.

Tara Oakley (10)

Bute House Preparatory School, Hammersmith

ARGH!

Her parents were gripping tightly onto the cliff. She tried to help but no, no, no. 'Argh!' screamed Alice. Her mum and dad raced up the stairs to her bedroom. 'What's the matter?' they exclaimed.
Alice whimpered aloud, 'It's too horrible to talk about,' and that was all they heard.

Sophie Beckitt (10)

Bute House Preparatory School, Hammersmith

THE GHOST ON HALLOWEEN

As I arrived at my favourite café it seemed deserted and gloomy. The chairs were stacked and cobwebs hung from the ceilings. Disappearing shadows crept down the dark corridors. 'Ghosts! Ghosts!' I screamed.
'Oooo,' replied the ghosts.
'Happy Halloween,' said a ghost, hoping to get some candy.
'Great Halloween costumes!'

Isabelle Lewitt (9)

Bute House Preparatory School, Hammersmith

THE LONELY PRINCESS

One day there was a princess called Georgia. She lived in a small cottage on her own. She was lonely. She went into the woods to get some berries. When she walked she met the frightening dragon. A prince came and killed the dragon! Then they got married!

Reanne Lee (7)

Finlay Community School, Gloucester

THE PRINCE, PRINCESS AND DRAGON

On a mountaintop there stood a castle with a prince and a princess. Then a fire-breathing dragon came along. Suddenly the dragon tried to capture the princess, to have her as a slave.
The prince came along to save the princess. They lived happily, peacefully, greatly ever after.

Alana Gardner-Michael (8)

Finlay Community School, Gloucester

THE DISASTER!

The two sisters packed for their holiday. 'Are you ready?' questioned Lily.
'Just checking I have everything.'
'Hurry up! The taxi is outside. It has beeped the horn three times already!'
They arrive at the airport, grab a coffee and sit down.
'Oh no! I've forgotten my passport!' shouted Melody.

Kaena Lewis (10)

Finlay Community School, Gloucester

THE DARK FOREST

One night a boy went to the dark forest. Suddenly he heard something breathing over him. Before he could turn around something grabbed hold of him, it was a wolf. It bit at his face but the boy hit him back and kicked him and then the wolf ran away.

Conor Moody
St James the Great RC Primary School, Thornton Heath

ZOMBIE HORROR

One day a child called Max went to the shop to buy some food for his parents. But when he went into the shop an alarm came on. The child was scared but when the alarm stopped a big frightened zombie came out of the ground and grabbed the boy.

Patryk Kopczyski
St James the Great RC Primary School, Thornton Heath

I DARE YOU

It's a stormy day and I'm playing dare with Ella. Finally it's my turn and I've dared Ella to go to the haunted house. I'd never do such a thing. Amazingly she goes.
Evening, and she's not back. I wonder where she is? Not in danger ... I hope!

Simona Tedros

St James the Great RC Primary School, Thornton Heath

THE BIG MONSTER

A little boy was playing in the garden by the trees. The boy heard a noise so the little boy turned around and he saw a big green monster. The monster stared at the little boy and gobbled him up. The monster said, 'That's good for my tummy.' *Burp, burp!*

Vienna Aplicella

St James the Great RC Primary School, Thornton Heath

THE SURPRISE

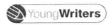

The house was nice and warm when my brother came home. 'What a nice time to put up the Christmas tree,' he said.
'Surprise!' shouted Mum and Dad. 'Have a look at this big wonderful Christmas tree.'
My brother and I were amazed. All of us were so happy.

Kaylin Fernandes (8)

St James the Great RC Primary School, Thornton Heath

UNTITLED

It was a dark gloomy night, I was in bed. Suddenly I heard a strange noise. I saw a pale face, I was terrified. I did not know what to do. The face came closer to me, jumped on my bed, it took off its mask. It was silly Ronald.

Jade Howard

St James the Great RC Primary School, Thornton Heath

THE CREAKING

The creaking was getting louder and louder, I was getting scared. What was I going to do? I heard it just outside the door. 'Dad!' I cried. 'Mum!' I cried. 'Help me quick, it is getting closer. I am going to die. Mum, help. Dad, help, please!'
'Yes, son!'
'You!'

Lewis Brennan (8)

St James the Great RC Primary School, Thornton Heath

THE HORROR HOUSE SHADOWS

Rose walked to the gates of Skullytop Hill. On the hill was a house, her friends called it the 'Horror House'. The gates creaked open, Rose slowly walked up to the house. Suddenly, screams and shouts came from the house. All was still now, Rose darted back home in horror.

Natalia Jimenez (9)

St James the Great RC Primary School, Thornton Heath

FABRIZIO!

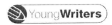

I couldn't get to sleep because I could hear a creaking sound. I went to see what it was. It was a Christmas tree. It took me and hung me like a ball. It told me that I would die.
I woke up, realising Fabrizio was making the noise.

Natalya Pereira (9)

St James the Great RC Primary School, Thornton Heath

ONE SUNNY DAY

One sunny day, Bob went to the park to see his friend, Mike. They played football. Mike shot five goals, Bob shot six. They both went to get ice cream. Bob had chocolate and Mike had strawberry. Bob hated strawberry and Mike hated chocolate. They both went home.

Terenzo Dino Lanzalaco (8)

St James the Great RC Primary School, Thornton Heath

PRINCESS UGLY AND HER LOST PRINCE

When Prince Charming heard that Princess Ugly was trapped, he galloped off to save her, but when he chopped down all the flowers and kissed her, she was already awake. She tried to make herself look pretty but it didn't work. So, they never ever lived happily ever after.

Lauren McLean (8)

St James the Great RC Primary School, Thornton Heath

THE BIG SNAKE

The snake was flicking its tongue. The snake was catching its prey. Its eyes gleaming in the night. Its fangs dripping with human blood. The snake squeezing on a tree. Its scales shone like the moon. Its skin was as green and slimy as a toffee bar. It was disgusting.

Zarion Brunton (9)

St James the Great RC Primary School, Thornton Heath

CAGED

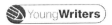

I'm creeping downstairs. There's an Amazon warrior in my small cottage. She appears fierce. I'm proceeding inside. She grabs me. Pushes me down a deep, dark hole. I see my mother, she's purple. I see a gleaming cage. I try running. Then I realise I am trapped, never to escape ...

Saskia Poulter (9)

St James the Great RC Primary School, Thornton Heath

THE HOUSE GOES BANG!

One day I was walking a long path and I heard a bang. I noticed that a house was on fire and so I went and looked there. My back caught fire so I ran away and jumped into a lake. It was all OK.

Matthew Madine

St James the Great RC Primary School, Thornton Heath

THE ADVENTURE STORY

One day I found a key, immediately it took me to another world. I started walking then I saw something. I started to run then I tripped over a twig. It got closer, I carried on running, then I remembered the key. I could go back to Earth.

Massimo Wheeler
St James the Great RC Primary School, Thornton Heath

THE HORRIFYING HALLOWEEN STORY

A girl heard a creak, the girl was walking downstairs. She saw a coffin. She was very frightened and scared. She tried to open the coffin but she was looking at it, even staring. She opened the coffin, a skeleton appeared, blood was dripping ... Her brother laughed and laughed.

David Akpani (8)
St James the Great RC Primary School, Thornton Heath

THE BIG LIZARD

The lizard was big, it slept in a house. The boy tried to touch it but it bit him. The lizard climbed on his back. It was swiping its claws at the boy's neck. It hurt the boy. He tried to pull it but it kept on swiping him.

Michael Cotzias (8)

St James the Great RC Primary School, Thornton Heath

THE TWO BOYS WHO GOT KIDNAPPED

One day, me and my friend were walking down the street to get an ice cream. When we got there we saw a man with a black mask. We felt scared and we ran to my house. We opened the door, then I saw the man and he got us.

Jaden Daway

St James the Great RC Primary School, Thornton Heath

THE COLD ONE

Charlotte went into a scary house. A ghostly-like figure rushed up to her at the speed of light. 'Who are you? What are you?' The ghost soon looked human. She touched it, *so cold,* her thoughts told her, *do not worry, you will soon be friends.* 'So cold, Brrr!'

Mya Henry (10)

St James the Great RC Primary School, Thornton Heath

JIMMY AND THE DREAM

One day, a boy named Jimmy moved into a haunted house.

That night, in his bedroom, he saw something in the mirror. When he looked there was nothing there. The hair on his neck stood with fear. He could smell something burning. It was his mum burning the toast!

Erika McKeon (9)

St James the Great RC Primary School, Thornton Heath

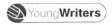

THE HORROR WITHIN

The dark jungle towered over me, there were eerie sounds coming from within. I ventured in to investigate. It was pitch-black, I couldn't see anything. Suddenly, there was a crack behind me, I spun around shouting, 'Show yourself.' Then there was a growl and I ran for my life.

Niall Byrne (10)

St James the Great RC Primary School, Thornton Heath

THE SCREAM

Strolling across the green grass Lilly came to a big purple house with bats flying around it. She knocked on the door and it opened by itself. She shouted, 'Hello? Hello?' but no one answered. The door closed right before her eyes. She screamed, but no one heard her ...

Melissa Noel

St James the Great RC Primary School, Thornton Heath

TITANIC

'Danger ahead,' Captain said.
Noble Jack steered the ship, dodging all the icebergs. It was very foggy. The waves crashed about. An iceberg in front knocked them down. They washed away to waste, sunk and that was the end of them. They fell to a perishing death; failing their mission.

Joshua Joseph (10)

St James the Great RC Primary School, Thornton Heath

MR MONKEY

Mr Monkey, up in a tree eating bananas and monkey nuts, chucking the leftovers down to the people below. People are screaming and people are shocked but Mr Monkey continues to stamp and stomp, giving the others a special surprise.

Charlotte Jones (10)

St James the Great RC Primary School, Thornton Heath

THE BOGEYMAN

'Argh!' Oh no, it's all happening, everything I am scared of! He's here, the horrendous monster that has been visiting me in my sleep. He has been in my dreams, scaring me all month. He is staring at me with his dagger eyes. 'Who are you?'
'I am the bogeyman!'

Lorna Behan (11)
St James the Great RC Primary School, Thornton Heath

HOLIDAY ADVENTURES

It was 9 o'clock and there was a terrifying scream echoing through the cave. A ten-year-old girl called Vanessa walked through the cave. The ground was as dry as the Sahara Desert and there were dirty evil bats around and guess what was in front of her face ... ?

Nathan Akpani (10)
St James the Great RC Primary School, Thornton Heath

A DAY IN THE LIFE OF AN ANIMAL

The sun hit me like a flash of lightning. No water in the watering hole. Not one tree in sight. Our family dying of thirst. Our backs drooping. Finally a shady tree. My body hit the floor like a giant drum. I closed my eyes and never woke up.

Jodie Howard (11)

St James the Great RC Primary School, Thornton Heath

WHY DID I RUN AWAY?

Whoosh, woo, chitter-chatter, my teeth chattered as the furious wind hit my face. I wished I'd never run away from home. In the park, the spindly branches of trees snapped like daggers trying to pierce me through the heart.

Suddenly, I heard footsteps coming towards me. What was it?

Gemma Blundell-Doyle (10)

St James the Great RC Primary School, Thornton Heath

HOLIDAY ADVENTURE

Rain pouring buckets! I am the only boy amongst these girls. We need to go back home. So desperate to get shelter. A few more hours until pitch-black. Can't make it home with a small bit of petrol left. 'Split up. Search for help.'
'Hurry! Darkness is creeping up.'

Rhianne Creary (10)

St James the Great RC Primary School, Thornton Heath

THE SHADOW

It was eerily tense, like the gloomy room was holding its breath. Suddenly a gigantic shadow towered over me. I stumbled backwards, my eyes agitated and scared. I slowly glanced down and a hilarious sight greeted me. The small puppy shuffled awkwardly away. I laughed and shook my relieved head.

Sean Cobb (10)

St James the Great RC Primary School, Thornton Heath

THE BEAST IS AFTER ME

Darkness everywhere! I reached home at 7pm, the house was silent. I expected my mum to be home. My name was being screamed from the attic. 'Jack? Jack?' Coldness rushed though my body. I went to the cold, dusty attic, the moonlight shone through the window. The beast got me.

Immanuel Opong Mills (11)

St James the Great RC Primary School, Thornton Heath

SILENCE SPEAKS LOUDER THAN WORDS

The tension was thick enough to cut through with a knife. Even the dilapidated brown axe in Jacob's hands wasn't enough to quell his fear. With trembling hands, the scrawny adolescent opened the creaky door slightly to reveal ...

Rory Taylor

St James the Great RC Primary School, Thornton Heath

WHERE ARE YOUR TAILS?

'Your tails have been cut off,' Little Bo Peep chuckled when her sheep came home. They had left their tails behind them. Little Bo Peep could not stop giggling. All was nice. The hot sunlight beamed on Little Bo Peep's pink blushing cheeks, until there was a loud ... 'Cut!'

Rebecca Adrianne Goulding (10)
St James the Great RC Primary School, Thornton Heath

THE STAIRS

Ding-dong. It was midnight. I headed home. *Howl.* I started to run home, terrified. I twisted the key into the lock and entered. I switched on the television. *Creak.* The first time I thought nothing of it. *Creak.* I looked around and saw something lurking on the stairs. 'Argh!'

Annie Vella (10)
St James the Great RC Primary School, Thornton Heath

HOME ALONE AND A BIG BANG FROM THE ATTIC

Bang! Amelia heard a noise coming from the cold, dark attic! 'What can that noise be?'
Amelia ran upstairs, hoping it wasn't anything big and terrifying. She reached for the doorknob. 'What can this noise be?' She hadn't heard it before. 'What shall I do!' She opened the door ...

Charlotte Allen (10)

St James the Great RC Primary School, Thornton Heath

GHOSTLY GOINGS-ON

A creepy groan stretched down the deserted, crumbling alleyway filling Tom with ghastly thoughts of his ghostly past. He picked up the pace and started to quickly scurry down the haunted alleyway. There he saw it, floating. 'Argh!' He quivered in fear and shut his eyes. It was gone!

Charles Desa (11)

St James the Great RC Primary School, Thornton Heath

PELELIU

Bang! Bombs exploding, bullets flying on this blasted beach! We had landed on the Peleliu beach. It was full of mines and barbed wire. The corpses littered the beach head. Crimson blood was flying everywhere. I landed with my squad. Machine guns fired. I hit the beach. *Bang!* Dead.

Sean Goswell (11)

St James the Great RC Primary School, Thornton Heath

WHAT HAS HAPPENED?

'Help!' I hear as I enter my house. My shopping drops. I rush upstairs, I hear a splat and look down. I see a pool of blood rushing down. I get upstairs and see a body as pale as a cloud. 'Help!' I scream!

Osadebamwen Ojo-Osagie (10)

St James the Great RC Primary School, Thornton Heath

THE HUMOROUS GHOST

Bong! the gigantic grandfather clock chimed loudly as I skipped up the steep creaky stairs at midnight in my haunted castle. Suddenly a cold shiver ran down my spine. I saw a ghostly shadow waiting for me outside my bedroom door. He threw feathers over me and shouted, 'Got you!'

Olamide Olufemi-Krakue (10)

St James the Great RC Primary School, Thornton Heath

THE FUNNY GHOST

Smash! the grandfather clock chimed as I walked up the steep, creaky stairs at midnight, in my haunted mansion. Suddenly a cold shiver ran down my spine. I saw a ghostly shadow waiting for me outside my bedroom door. He threw slime at me as he shouted loudly, 'Got you!'

Amanda Burrows (10)

St James the Great RC Primary School, Thornton Heath

CAVE MONSTER

The people on the street ran past the Leaning Tower of Pisa. I darted off towards a cave and entered to see the beast standing before me. Speedily I drew my sword and slashed its stomach but it just healed. I removed my lightning bolt and struck it. Victory!

Alexander Szymaniak (8)
St James the Great RC Primary School, Thornton Heath

MY ADVENTURE

I came face to face with the Kalo in the Underworld. The Kalo looked like he was going to explode when he mis-kicked me. Suddenly I plunged my sword into his heart. The Kalo was dead and I saved my beloved Charlie, who I set out to get back.

Joe Harries (8)
St James the Great RC Primary School, Thornton Heath

JACK

One day, Jack sprinted, as he went, he left all of his friends. Zarton stole Jack's blue ruby. Jack was going to get the ruby.
Jack got to Zarton's cave and used his power sword. Jack killed Zarton by cutting his tail off. So Jack got his ruby back. Victory!

Conor O'Donovan (7)
St James the Great RC Primary School, Thornton Heath

THE HAUNTED HOUSE

Once upon a time there was a haunted house, there were people living there. Every night the ghost came out of its dark, creepy place. The people could not sleep. For one night the people were upset that they were in a very haunted house so they slew the ghost!

Racheal Largie-Poleon (7)
St James the Great RC Primary School, Thornton Heath

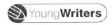

ANIMALS HAVING FUN

It was a sunny day. Molly and the dolphins were playing together. *Splash! Splash!* The dolphins dived in the sea and they swam under the water. Suddenly they jumped out of the water. Then they saw more dolphins.

Mya Dixon (7)

St James the Great RC Primary School, Thornton Heath

EMILY'S BIRTHDAY

It was Emily's birthday on Friday the 8th October. Emily really wanted a phone, her mum couldn't afford a Blackberry. Emily said, 'Can I have a puppy as well?' Soon it was night-time so Emily went to bed.
Emily got all her presents the next morning.

Megan Batchelor (8)

St James the Great RC Primary School, Thornton Heath

THE GHOST HOUSE

Once upon a time there was a child called Lelho. He was scared about ghosts because he thought that they really existed. Every night he slept with his mom and dad.
One day it became true. Ghosts came out of his mum's cupboard. They woke up and ran ...

Antonio Bollito (7)

St James the Great RC Primary School, Thornton Heath

POOR LOCKY

Locky was flying in the sky. When he landed the children started to lick him. First his legs, then his tummy, then his wings. He tried to leave. He couldn't, his wings had gone! The only thing left was his cola-flavoured hair!

Francis Appiah (7)

St James the Great RC Primary School, Thornton Heath

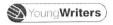

THE HAUNTED HOUSE

One day, there were two twins called Luke and Amy. They went to bed then suddenly a ghost came and went into Amy's head.
Amy woke up in the night and she screeched.
Her mum said, 'Don't be silly Amy, go back to bed!'

Sabina Ngatunga (7)
St James the Great RC Primary School, Thornton Heath

THE ADVENTURE

Amy and Adam went to the seaside. 'Mum, can I have my food now?' The wave blew it away. 'My sandwich, my sandwich,' shouted Amy in fear. Amy ran over the sea and nearly drowned. Adam went into the wavy sea and saved Amy. 'Thank you so much,' she said.

Antonio Dweben (7)
St James the Great RC Primary School, Thornton Heath

THE GREAT BIG GIANT

Under the dark night there was a heroine called Jamilla. Jamilla's mission was to kill the great nasty giant. Jamilla, the heroine, sprinted to the giant and shot arrows directly at the giant. But it wasn't dying. So she grabbed her super arrows out and he fell and died.

Sinead Obeng (7)
St James the Great RC Primary School, Thornton Heath

THE DEATH OF THE WORM

The ice was gleaming when Jakub jumped into a gigantic worm's lair underground. Jakub ran to get a potion that said, 'Danger! Kills me!' Jakub grabbed the potion and threw it in the gigantic worm's mouth. It killed the worm.

Eleanor O'Regan (7)
St James the Great RC Primary School, Thornton Heath

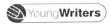

THE BEAST OF THE THREE CAVES

There was a girl called Halley who was babysitting. Abby had been stolen. Halley followed footprints to the three caves. Inside the three caves there was a beast with poisonous nails. Halley ran for water to kill it. She threw water at it. It was gone.

Elle McGing (7)
St James the Great RC Primary School, Thornton Heath

ISABELLA AND THE MONSTER

Lots of people gathered to buy food. Isabella dangerously ran across the rocky desert. She turned her head sharply and saw a ferocious monster. It was nibbling on children. Creeping, she grabbed a sharp sword and pierced the sharp sword into the monster's heart. He died. Isabella won the battle!

Renee Okeke (7)
St James the Great RC Primary School, Thornton Heath

MUD MONSTER

I was walking along until I heard a scream. I asked an old man what happened. 'It's the mud monster throwing trash!' replied the man.
'What?' I answered.
'Nothing,' said the man.
I crept behind the monster and dug holes in the ground. It stepped back and fell in. 'Hooray!'

Zarish Alban (7)

St James the Great RC Primary School, Thornton Heath

THE GIANT OCTOPUS

It was Saturday afternoon and I was at the beach. I heard a big wave, louder than ever. A piece of seaweed landed in front of me. It go bigger. It was an octopus. In my hand appeared a sword. I ran in the sea and stabbed the octopus. Victory!

Sarah Vella (8)

St James the Great RC Primary School, Thornton Heath

SNOWMEN THIEVES

One snowy night it was Christmas. The snowmen took all the presents for themselves. Ben wanted to have a good Christmas so he followed the snowmen to put them back. They didn't so Ben put some potion on them and they put them back exactly where they belonged.

Chidimma Muoghalu (7)
St James the Great RC Primary School, Thornton Heath

THE GIANT SPIDER

In a dark, unknown area AJ went hiding behind the Statue of Liberty, hiding from a giant spider. Suddenly AJ realised the spider's scar. He got an old sword out and distracted the spider. AJ got bug spray and sprayed it at him.
New York said thanks. AJ lived happily.

Giovanni Demba-Martins (7)
St James the Great RC Primary School, Thornton Heath

CLAW ATTACK TO RED ALERT

I saw a sad, crying woman in a smelly stable. I went over to her and said, 'What did you lose?'
She said, 'My jewellery from a red panther.'
I jumped and tried to punch the panther but it dodged my fist. I then punched it, it died. Victory.

Alessandro MacKinnon-Botti (8)

St James the Great RC Primary School, Thornton Heath

BIG BEN'S GONE

Crazy crowds cramped London as the aftermath came. Madlin sprinted to a hole and jumped down. Armed with tomato ketchup, Madlin ran into the lair. She saw Big Ben! The monster was there. Madlin squirted tomato ketchup at the monster. Victory!

Molly Murphy (7)

St James the Great RC Primary School, Thornton Heath

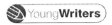

THE MAN AND HIS KNIFE

Benny came home. He saw something glisten in the moonlight, a red liquid slithered down the stairs. Benny saw the guilt and terror on his face. Then, in his hand, a deadly knife. He stepped down the stairs at a slow pace. His body moved closer. Benny screamed in terror.

Karl Ramos (11)

St James the Great RC Primary School, Thornton Heath

THE HOUSE WITH NOTHING INSIDE

As Bertie opened the creaking door of the terrifying haunted house, he could hear the rats scattering around the dusty floor and sneaky spiders lurking about in the darkness. Bertie was as frightened as if a spider was crawling down his back. Then Bertie heard a scream and zoomed away.

Johanna Lee (9)

St James the Great RC Primary School, Thornton Heath

THE FLYING MONKEY

The monkey called Lenny wanted to fly, but everyone knew monkeys couldn't fly. Everyone laughed. It was his dream but he wanted to stay cool so he thought, *I'll forget about my dream.*
Lenny was in a bad mood and was being creative. He made some wings and flew away!

Davey Newman (9)

St Joseph's Catholic Primary School, Chalfont St Peter

THE MAGIC BEAR

Lilly woke up on Christmas morning. Had he been? She woke her mum and dad and went downstairs. She loved her presents. She got loads, including a little fluffy white bear. She loved it. Suddenly, the bear came to life, winked then waved and they lived happily ... or not?

Rachel Broadley (9)

St Joseph's Catholic Primary School, Chalfont St Peter

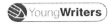

THE VERY BIG MISTAKE FROM SANTA

One night, Santa gave presents to everybody, even Mary and Joseph, but Santa put the wrong labels on the presents. Mary and Joseph got a teddy, and the little boy got a child, and so the boy and the child started to become friends. They next day they'd gone.

Paige Bailey (10)
St Joseph's Catholic Primary School, Chalfont St Peter

LIZARDS AND FLOODS IN GUAM

Once, there was a house on Guam. It was on the beach. At night lizards climbed into the house and ate the people's fingers.
In the morning all the people were dead except for one person. While she was eating lunch there was a flood and she died.

Hannah Topolosky (10)
St Joseph's Catholic Primary School, Chalfont St Peter

JACK FROST AND RAY RAIN

Jack Frost was wondering, should he make frost in the night when Sally Sunshine appeared. Jack said, 'Go away, Sally - I'm going to make lots of frost!'
'Oh yeah,' said Sally. 'I'll make it sunny!'
The next morning it was very wet as Ray Rain was annoyed with them arguing.

Finn Ruttledge (9)

St Joseph's Catholic Primary School, Chalfont St Peter

CHRISTMAS DAY

I woke up early that morning. It was Christmas Day. I crept down the stairs. I went to the living room. I saw my stocking, it was full to the top. Just then my parents came. 'Merry Christmas!'
I opened my present. I had got a DS, 'Brilliant!'

Elliot Potter (10)

St Joseph's Catholic Primary School, Chalfont St Peter

DIVE

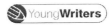

Bang! went the bullet as it was fired from the gun. I dived for cover but I was in the middle of nowhere. I saw the man who fired and went for him. He saw me coming, jumped in his car and drove off. I never ever saw him again.

Joshua Simpson (9)

St Joseph's Catholic Primary School, Chalfont St Peter

THE NIGHT SHE WOKE UP

She crept downstairs to get a drink, when she bumped into Santa. 'Hello little girl, you must be Lauren.'
'How do you know my name?' she asked.
'I know everything,' said Santa. 'I have a present for you.'
'Thanks!' she said and crept back to bed. 'Did I dream it?'

Erin Moore (10)

St Joseph's Catholic Primary School, Chalfont St Peter

APRIL FOOLS

Jemma walked into the living room. There was a long silence while they were all sitting down. Her father broke the tension, 'Jemma we're leaving London. We are going to Austria!'
She felt like the ground was going to swallow her up, but then ...
'Only Joking! April Fools!' they chorused.

Selena McGuinness (10)
St Joseph's Catholic Primary School, Chalfont St Peter

THE DAY TO REMEMBER!

Today I went to the Sea Life park, it was amazing. I saw shiny starfish, clippy crabs, dazzling dolphins and raving rays. The park owner said I was allowed to touch the rays and starfish.
I saw many things that day. It was a day to remember!

Emily-Ann Johnson (10)
St Joseph's Catholic Primary School, Chalfont St Peter

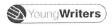

THE MYSTERIOUS LODGER

The new lodger came into the flat. He looked very suspicious and shifty. The landlady, Mrs Grimpen, did not look too pleased. 'Well, are you my new lodger? Where is my money then? Come on, cough it up!'
All of a sudden the new lodger shot and Mrs Grimpen died.

Lucy Harrison (10)

St Joseph's Catholic Primary School, Chalfont St Peter

THE NIGHT BEFORE CHRISTMAS

It was the night before Christmas and everyone was excited. One family wasn't, they were dull and boring. People called them the 'Funsuckers'.
After Christmas they were the total opposite. They never wanted it to end because all the village started boasting so they decorated the entire village.

Sophie Gilsoon (9)

St Joseph's Catholic Primary School, Chalfont St Peter

ALONG THE DIRT TRACK

He was running in the heat of the day, along the dirt track. His heart was pounding as sweat flowed down his bright red cheeks. He could hear the approaching car closer now. He took a split second to look back and heard a *bang,* then suddenly he fell down.

Hannah Poulter (9)

St Joseph's Catholic Primary School, Chalfont St Peter

A DREAM

One night there were two children and their father in a car. They were called Alice, Jasper and John. Then suddenly John fainted. Alice said, 'Jasper, come on, you know how to drive.'

Jasper replied, 'Fine.'

Then suddenly Alice heard a noise. 'It was just a dream,' she said, relieved.

Kiara Hussein (9)

St Joseph's Catholic Primary School, Chalfont St Peter

THE GHOST TEDDY

Paul screamed in his sleep and Dad came in to see what was wrong. 'I can't find my teddy. It must be a ghost.'
Mum came running in with his teddy. 'I washed it for you as a surprise,' she said.
'Yay,' Paul said and he went back to sleep.

Marco Petrosino (10)
St Joseph's Catholic Primary School, Chalfont St Peter

A BAD DAY WITH A STRANGER

Arthur Dent and a stranger have been arguing on this strange and unusual planet. 'It's just this guy you know.'
'What guy?'
'That guy!' and then he pointed and what stood in front of them was a giant monster!
'Yeah, it is just a guy,' and then Arthur Dent fainted.

Liam McGuinness (9)
St Joseph's Catholic Primary School, Chalfont St Peter

HAPPY BIRTHDAY!

It was Susie's big day, she was turning sixteen and was looking forward to the sixth hour when her big party started. She was hoping she would get an amazing main present, an Amazon Kindle or a new mobile. The sixth hour approached. She opened the kitchen door. 'Happy sixteenth!'

Olivia Aldrich (10)

St Joseph's Catholic Primary School, Chalfont St Peter

THE WOODS

Once upon a time there was a girl who lived in a house next to the woods. It was very dark so no one lived there and every day she wondered if there was anything there.

One night she went there and she found treasure. But was it?

Nimren Kaur Khaira (9)

St Joseph's Catholic Primary School, Chalfont St Peter

THE DREAM

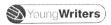

Laura sat on the edge of the steep cliff. Looking down, she felt afraid and nervous. Her heart was beating fast, below were her parents shouting, 'Laura, don't jump. Help is on its way.'
Suddenly, Laura was falling to the ground, then she woke up. It was all a dream.

Tara McGrory White (10)
St Joseph's Catholic Primary School, Chalfont St Peter

THE DEADLY SHARK

Under the water of the deep blue sea was a frightened little boy, struggling to breathe. People were out looking for him. He could never survive without air.
The young boy came into view when suddenly, a huge shark appeared out of nowhere. The boy was never seen again.

Jessica Glover (10)
St Joseph's Catholic Primary School, Chalfont St Peter

THE STORY OF THE TITANIC

The Titanic had been boarded. The ship set sail. They hit an invisible iceberg. The ship flooded, people screamed. The boat began to sink. The water was very cold. More people screamed some people jumped off. Bye-bye so-called indestructible ship. No, a boring old rotten chunk of ice.

Kieron Jones (10)

St Joseph's Catholic Primary School, Chalfont St Peter

RED ALERT

'Doctor, doctor, the patient's red alert!'
I opened my eyes. No one seemed to notice. Was I in a hospital? Why? I suddenly felt my strength ebbing away. Someone was still speaking, 'We believed that the haemorrhaging had stopped. We were wrong.'
Those were the last words that I heard ...

Alex Ortega (10)

St Joseph's Catholic Primary School, Chalfont St Peter

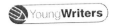

LET IT SNOW, LET IT SNOW, LET IT SNOW

One cold winter's day it was chucking it down with snow. Nobody could get out of their homes.
The next morning rescuers had to come and move all of the snow, right outside the people's houses.
Finally everybody was safe from the snow. Everyone was very, very, very happy.

Meg Harrigan (10)

St Joseph's Catholic Primary School, Chalfont St Peter

DRAGON!

Long ago, in a faraway land, there was a boy called Ben. Ben lived in Veromophia, everything was tranquil there, but ... *Roar!* Oh no, they had some problems. *Dragons!* Ben wanted to tame these dragons so he went up and tamed the dragons.
After that everything was peaceful.

Connor Conaty (10)

St Joseph's Catholic Primary School, Chalfont St Peter

DEATH TREE

On Christmas Eve a young boy called Ben Jackson Jones was sleeping when he heard a loud crash. He went downstairs to see that his tree had come to life. It was destroying everything and was setting up some dynamite. Ben stood there in shock. The tree said, 'Bye!' *Boom!*

Emilio Trillo (11)

St Joseph's Catholic Primary School, Chalfont St Peter

THE CHRISTMAS TREE

One snowy Christmas Day a boy named Lewis and a very dull father named Max decided to make a Christmas tree. But, the very dull father decided to sleep instead! So while Max was asleep, Lewis made the most amazing tree ever, with shiny baubles and sparkly lights.

James Hamberger (11)

St Joseph's Catholic Primary School, Chalfont St Peter

UNTITLED

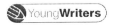

'Come on team, we can win this even though we are 1-0 down. We can still come back and win this because we have a penalty. If we score it'll be 1-1 and then we could still win.'
'1-1 and it is full-time! What a result. 1-1 - yes!'

Ben Woodward (10)
St Joseph's Catholic Primary School, Chalfont St Peter

ARMY OF UNDEAD!

One night, when the army of the undead were rising, one little boy called Nathan was walking along the pavement when he saw a shadow, a large pitch-black shadow of evil ... Just then Nathan was swallowed whole. The shadow was a monster with devil horns. It was back, haunting.

Chinecherem Atrtama (11)
St Joseph's Catholic Primary School, Chalfont St Peter

WORLD AT WAR

'Get down, get down,' as a long hairy fang came down. William said, 'Get ready to run boys. Run!' As a fang killed millions of people, as the army took out their guns and opened fire, as they jumped into the dark and blackened mystery pit, never to be seen again.

Tiarnan Greene (11)

St Joseph's Catholic Primary School, Chalfont St Peter

THE EMBARRASSING PARENT

As the moon was brewing, a young boy and his girlfriend went out for dinner. Then the young boy's mother and father turned up at the restaurant and sat on the reserved table next to the young boy and girl and started to blabber about how cute he was.

Elley-May Mackenzie (10)

St Joseph's Catholic Primary School, Chalfont St Peter

FISHWORLD

One day, there was a young goldfish called Flash. He was a hero to his tank. You will find out why.
'Listen fishy, give me your money,' yelled a nasty shrimp.
'Here you go,' shivered a scared little fish.
'No give the money back.'
'Fine.'
'Thank you Flash.'
'You're welcome.'

Lewis Gray (10)

St Joseph's Catholic Primary School, Chalfont St Peter

SNOW

Sophie was sitting on the stairs, cold as ice. The house was damp and cold. The stairs were creaking. She was all alone. Then a *knock-knock.* Sophie gave a start. There it was again, that knocking. The door creaked open. Snow, beautiful snow, flooded in. She rushed out. 'Snow!'

Orla Bentley (10)

St Joseph's Catholic Primary School, Chalfont St Peter

UGLY, TERRIFYING MONSTER

'Run! It's an ugly, terrifying monster. It's going to munch us!'

'It's heading to the ice cream shop and the entertainment store, also the bundle cheap sweet shop and the video game store. Nooo! It's coming to our house. We've got to do something. Let's call the police, they'll know.'

Joshua James (10)

St Joseph's Catholic Primary School, Chalfont St Peter

MY BIRTHDAY

On my birthday, I woke up to, 'Happy birthday to you!' It was my parents. I had breakfast in bed, then I went downstairs to open my presents. I opened all my presents in a hurry; they were all boring. Then I found another, it was just what I wanted.

Joseph Derry (10)

St Joseph's Catholic Primary School, Chalfont St Peter

MONA LISA FAKE

As John went to the loft to get down the Christmas decorations, he saw, in the corner, a painting that looked just like the Mona Lisa.
The next morning, he went to some art experts.
'It's definitely very interesting. Wait a second, it's real!' they said.
John then slowly fainted.

James Wroe (10)
St Joseph's Catholic Primary School, Chalfont St Peter

LAST DAY

She opened a coffin and somebody pushed her. 'Argh!' a voice screamed horribly. 'Ha, ha!' said the horrible wicked witch.
'You monster!' cried the little girl who got pushed.
'You will stay in here forever but will not die,' said the horrible wicked witch.

Max Harris (10)
St Joseph's Catholic Primary School, Chalfont St Peter

COLD CHRISTMAS

It was one very cold day on the 24th December 2010. It was snowing. All the children looked outside and said, 'It's snowed!'
After they had sent lists they got ready to go outside with nice warm clothes, hats, coats, scarves and gloves!

Connie Chana (10)

St Joseph's Catholic Primary School, Chalfont St Peter

THE BULLY

The teenage girl just walked in when the school bully came in. The teenager didn't know what to do, so she hid behind the door. The bully found her and beat her up. Luckily, the teacher came in. The school bully would no more bully anyone ever, ever, ever again.

Lydia Roberts (9)

St Joseph's Catholic Primary School, Chalfont St Peter

NIGHTMARE!

It's the day of the cup final. We all clambered onto the coach and the atmosphere was buzzing. Suddenly the coach came to a halt. 'Sorry boys,' cried the driver, 'we've broken down.'
'Oh no!'
Then I heard Mum's voice. 'Joseph, wake up, Cup Final day.'
'Phew, what a dream!'

Joseph Anthony (10)
St Joseph's Catholic Primary School, Chalfont St Peter

SCARED

As Toby opened the front door, a sudden misty shadow appeared in front of him. *Who could it be?* he thought anxiously. The figure let out its hand as if it was giving something. 'Argh!' screamed Toby.
'It's only me son,' said his dad. 'I went to do the shopping.'

Lauren Whight-Castillo (9)
St Joseph's Catholic Primary School, Chalfont St Peter

THE WAR SURPRISE

It was a dark and stormy night in the bomb shelter. All you could hear was the sound of the bombs and the little baby, Tim, crying. Then they heard a knock at the door. 'Come in,' said Kirsty excitedly.

At that moment their dad walked in. They were astounded.

Calumn Burrell (9)

St Joseph's Catholic Primary School, Chalfont St Peter

LILLY'S CHRISTMAS SURPRISE

One day, when Lilly went to school, it was cold and dark and she was sure school was on. She could hear banging and stamping from upstairs and the door burst open. Her school friends were there with presents and cards. What a really, really fun Christmas surprise.

Annie Morris (9)

St Joseph's Catholic Primary School, Chalfont St Peter

JUST ANOTHER SCHOOL DAY?

'Wake up!' shouted Mum.
Bleary-eyed Joe begrudgingly left his warm cosy bed. He yawned, wiping the sleep from his eyes. He tugged open his curtains. 'Snow!' he yelped. It blanketed everything, his previously green garden, now an alpine scene. Then suddenly it occurred to him. 'No school today, brilliant!'

James Woakes (10)
St Joseph's Catholic Primary School, Chalfont St Peter

MARY'S WALK HOME

Mary was walking home, she had been waiting for the bus for hours now. She decided that she should just walk home, but that was a bad idea - it was a full moon. She didn't care, she was brave.
Mary heard a terrifying howling sound. An enormous dog came closer ...

Charlie O'Donnell (10)
St Joseph's Catholic Primary School, Chalfont St Peter

TUNNEL

The tunnel was ahead of me, I had butterflies in my tummy and all the shouting and cheering had disappeared. I could hear nothing. I was really excited and then we began to move. My fears removed, we were out on the pitch ready to start my first Premiership match.

Mark McGuinness (9)

St Joseph's Catholic Primary School, Chalfont St Peter

THE START OF CHRISTMAS

Yesterday Daddy put the lights on the house. Then we got the tree and the decorations from the loft in the garage. As a family we started to put the tree up, with Christmas music in the background. Our lounge looked sparkly. Christmas was definitely coming home. But no snow!

Kennedy Newbert (9)

St Joseph's Catholic Primary School, Chalfont St Peter

THE PARTY

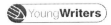

'Mum, we're nearly there at Lacey's party,' said Kayla. 'There it is.'
'Be careful,' argued Mum.
'Come in, Kayla,' exclaimed Lacey.
They entered the building, went up the stairs, got lost, they heard a scream. They were terrified then the door opened. It was Lacey's mum saving them.

Sophie Creighton (9)
St Joseph's Catholic Primary School, Chalfont St Peter

JADE'S SURPRISE

'Come to the party with me, won't you?' said Dylan.
'Sure!' said Jade.
They walked and walked and walked and ran. 'Where is it?' asked Jade.
'Just in here, Jade,' said Dylan.
Jade and Dylan stepped inside.
'Happy birthday!' shouted everyone.
'You shouldn't have!' shouted Jade. She was so happy!

Olivia McGee (9)
St Joseph's Catholic Primary School, Chalfont St Peter

BIG BANANA

I was in Greece, in the middle of the beach, waiting for a big banana. I found the big banana with my brother. Got on the front with my brother behind me. It started really slow. I felt weird. It got really fast. I felt happy. Then sadly it ended.

Elliott Williams (9)

St Joseph's Catholic Primary School, Chalfont St Peter

THE ATTACK

Matt woke up in a silent house. There was an eerie silence about the place. Suddenly a man burst in, 'You are of the five! You must be killed,' he hissed. Suddenly his skin fell off. He became a werewolf. The creature burst into pieces. Matt knew he did it!

Christian Jarcheh (10)

St Joseph's Catholic Primary School, Chalfont St Peter

FAIRIES?

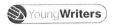

I love fairies. It's my birthday tomorrow, May 12th. What would I get? I couldn't wait.
Next day, I heard knocking on the door. There were savage beasts with bloody teeth. I reached my gun and pulled the trigger. Soon I started hunting them down. All the evil fairies. Dead!

James Doherty (10)

St Joseph's Catholic Primary School, Chalfont St Peter

THE OLD FARM

That night Harry was spying on his schoolmates. What he didn't know was that he was being followed.
Harry ran up to an old barn, suddenly a brick came through the window, hitting the barn wall. Harry ran but the barn fell, squashing him to death.

Max Gregory (11)

St Joseph's Catholic Primary School, Chalfont St Peter

A CHILD'S FOOTBALL DREAM

A child had a dream, it was to be a professional footballer. He would practise every time he got a ball. It was hard to play with his mum passing away.
It was the Champions League Final but his dad died. He swore he would never play football again!

Ciaran Boyle (10)

St Joseph's Catholic Primary School, Chalfont St Peter

ENDLESS DEATH

Under rock and blood lay Emma's father. Whilst in the south of Asia the daughter herself lay in hospital, from the sprained ankle caused by her tragic accident of falling down the stairs on her 10th birthday! Still poor Emma didn't know about her father's tragic death, until the end!

Olivia Rodriguez (11)

St Joseph's Catholic Primary School, Chalfont St Peter

SHOT AND GONE

It was the 13th of October. The sky was pitch-black and wolves howled. My friend and I were driving home, suddenly we stopped. My friend didn't stop the car but someone else did. I turned away and looked at my friend. My friend had gone and was shot dead.

Francesco Stanco (11)

St Joseph's Catholic Primary School, Chalfont St Peter

ALAN THE MESSENGER

It was raining around the castle. Alan was watching the fields and saw an army approaching. He sounded the alarms and rushed into the castle where the king was. He pushed the door open and found the king lying on his throne with an arrow in his chest.

Michael Lathrope (11)

St Joseph's Catholic Primary School, Chalfont St Peter

DESERTED

When I arrived home the lights were off and there was a strange noise coming from the kitchen. I went inside to check and I was greeted by a long bony hand. It swiped and it hit me. I fell to the ground with blood pulsing out of my stomach.

Joshua Roberts (10)

St Joseph's Catholic Primary School, Chalfont St Peter

CAMPING SURPRISE

Velma, Daphne and Frederic went on holiday to camp for the night. In the middle of the night they heard a crunching sound and imagined that it was a monster. Then Daphne looked outside the tent and saw a poor hungry rabbit, so Daphne gave him a big juicy carrot.

Susannah Kiely (11)

St Joseph's Catholic Primary School, Chalfont St Peter

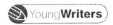

THE BIG ADVENTURE

One day in the UK, three brothers called Tom, Josh and Pablo were going to Japan on a plane. When they arrived in Japan they got a taxi to Tokyo to their uncle's house. When they opened the creepy door, they found a note, it said: 'We've got your uncle'.

Pablo Brown (10)

St Joseph's Catholic Primary School, Chalfont St Peter

THE DARKNESS

It was a dark night in Chalfont, there was a power cut. I looked out of the window, there lay my uncle, my dad and my baby brother.
Two hours later, I was thinking, *am I the last one?* Suddenly the power came back on ... I saw a witch, 'Noooo!'

Callum Farrell (10)

St Joseph's Catholic Primary School, Chalfont St Peter

DIARY OF ROBSON GREEN - WORLD WAR II

It was the same day in the dirty old trench, me and my best friend ran out, fired our Tommy guns and blew the Germans' heads off. I threw a frag in a building but seconds later ... Banzai attack, screaming, shouting all around us and *boom!* My friend was gone.

Alex Jones (10)

St Joseph's Catholic Primary School, Chalfont St Peter

ERUPTION

A loud bang erupted behind me. I ricocheted off the wall and collapsed. I woke up Tom who was lying there - in the middle of the road. I looked down, there were thousands of splinters in my legs. 'Tom,' I called out weakly. It was too late.

Euan Williams (10)

St Joseph's Catholic Primary School, Chalfont St Peter

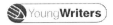

DISASTER STRIKES

One dark, cold night, in the town of Amble, there was lightning. Suddenly, the lightning hit a telephone wire tower and knocked down three houses. It killed over 100 people, five dogs, two cats and eight guinea pigs.

Riley Ashe (11)
St Joseph's Catholic Primary School, Chalfont St Peter

MURDER MYSTERY

Suddenly, there was a loud scream. I ran downstairs to see what it was. I looked in the living room, nothing. I peeked into the kitchen, to find my son lying on the floor. First I didn't know what to think of it, but then I realised what happened.

Lily McMahon (10)
St Joseph's Catholic Primary School, Chalfont St Peter

BUT IT'S CHRISTMAS EVE

'Come and put your stockings up,' said Mum. 'Hurry up!'
Their dad was an air raid warden and was on call. They were about to put them up when they heard the air raid siren.
'Sorry but I've got to go,' said Dad.
'But it's Christmas Eve, Dad!'

Josie Coyle (10)

St Joseph's Catholic Primary School, Chalfont St Peter

THE BATTLE!

George, in battle, fighting for survival. He finally drew the sword against the dragon's chest. His heart thumped heavily. He stabbed the dragon, puncturing his body. All he saw was blood pulsing, pouring out onto the craggy rocks. He took a sigh of relief. Everyone cheered. The dragon was dead.

Maisie Morris (11)

St Joseph's Catholic Primary School, Chalfont St Peter

SURPRISE!

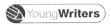

'Quick!' said my sister. 'It's here!'
I jumped out of bed and ran to the window, opened the curtains and there, as far as I could see, just within my reach. I thought it was a dream, a dream everyone had been waiting for. A blanket of pure white snow!

Francesca Wallace (8)

St Joseph's Catholic Primary School, Haywards Heath

DAISY

It was an unusually busy day for Daisy and the phone just kept ringing as she was mixing hair dye. She squirted a big dollop into the bowl, gave it a mix and applied it to Miss Rose's hair. She left it for ten minutes, then checked the colour. *Disaster!*

Harriet Garvey (7)

St Joseph's Catholic Primary School, Haywards Heath

GHOST TRAIN

I entered the exhilarating theme park called 'The Ghastly Ghosts'. I was the first one on the frightening ghost train and, surprisingly, I was alone. Suddenly, I knew why, the sound of a flood came rushing. I was falling to my death, I shouted, 'Help!'

Michael Crummey (10)
St Joseph's Catholic Primary School, Haywards Heath

UNTITLED

One day a boy called Edd was searching for his rucksack up in the attic. Suddenly a trail of creaky footsteps surrounded him ... the door slammed behind him, then suddenly ... something made him shiver, he closed his eyes, the sounds stopped. He opened them, he was in bed, dreaming.

Sam Paton (10)
St Joseph's Catholic Primary School, Haywards Heath

THE BIG BIRTHDAY SURPRISE

'Out the way,' shouted the burglars, they ran into Leon's house. Leon ran into his house and looked all around, then suddenly more burglars came in with wrapped up things. Leon did not know what to do. He went in and … 'Happy birthday!' Leon was happy.

Leon Holiness (10)

St Joseph's Catholic Primary School, Haywards Heath

A FLUFFY TAIL

'Olivia! Olivia!' I shouted excitedly. 'Come and look!' Olivia ran over to the mountain of autumn leaves.
'What?' she asked curiously.
'Can you hear it? Listen, there it is again,' I told her.
'Oh yeah! What do you think it is?'
Out popped a fluffy tail. My neighbour's dog. Fluffy!

Daniella Wallace (11)

St Joseph's Catholic Primary School, Haywards Heath

THE TRICK

It was a cold, dark day. Mary stood at the old, abandoned house. She creaked open the rusty door. She stepped in, a howling sound made her jump. Suddenly, a monster appeared in front of her. 'Argh!' she screamed.
'Mary?' came the monster. It was Carl. Mary felt very embarrassed.

Thomas Castel (10)
St Joseph's Catholic Primary School, Haywards Heath

IT WAS ALL A DREAM

I ran to the door as my vein was rushing. I heard a creak in the door, I felt frightened. I heard a noise nearby me, my heart beat. I felt like I was a scary, cold-blooded, horrible monster. All that I knew, it was all a silly dream.

Craig Flynn (10)
St Joseph's Catholic Primary School, Haywards Heath

WORLD CUP DREAM

There I was on the penalty spot. If I scored we would win the World Cup. I was under heaps of pressure. The ref blew the whistle. I ran up to take it. I scored. I did my favourite celebration. When I woke up, I said, 'Wow! What a dream!'

Sean Welsh (10)
St Joseph's Catholic Primary School, Haywards Heath

THOMAS AND THE TOADSTOOL PALACE

Thomas knocked on the fungus-covered door. He heard a creak come from inside. The door swung open and suddenly a bad stench blew into his face. Argh! Out jumped a great green monster.
Thomas picked up a stone. *Slap! Slurp! Ribbit! Click!* On went the lights. *A frog!*

Tyreece Andrews (10)
St Joseph's Catholic Primary School, Haywards Heath

WORLD CUP FINAL!

I was set, I was ready, the crowd were singing their hearts out and I walked onto the Wembley grass for the World Cup final against Brazil. The game was underway and I took a shot, I scored!
The early postman woke me up from a nice dream!

Charles Donohue (10)

St Joseph's Catholic Primary School, Haywards Heath

THE CREEPY LITTLE DOOR

There was a creepy little house in the town of Cuckfield. In that house lived a doctor. As soon as I was walking down the street I was tempted to go in. There were many heads, hanging from the walls. *Ding-dong!* The creepy little door opened!
'Trick or treat?'

Ernesto Paniccia (11)

St Joseph's Catholic Primary School, Haywards Heath

A LIFEGUARD'S DAY

Hello, I'm a lifeguard here in Lego City and ... *wawaw,* there's someone in trouble at sea! I'll get the boat.
'It's a shark and it's going to get that surfer!'
'Hey, it's a remote-controlled shark.'
Oops, never mind, I wonder when there is going to be a real emergency?

Theo Garraway (11)

St Joseph's Catholic Primary School, Haywards Heath

HOLIDAY SURPRISE

Suddenly I woke up with a start, and all my friends and family were right next to me. They all had a wonderful surprise for me.
'We're going to take you on holiday!'
'Yippee!' I shouted at the top of my voice. 'I have been waiting for this moment!'

Matthew Bacon (10)

St Joseph's Catholic Primary School, Haywards Heath

NIGHT OF HORROR!

On her way home from school, in the dark night, she leant over to the lamppost and she felt red water on her hand! Suddenly, when she got home she heard a *ding-dong!* Slowly she opened the door, there was no one there. Then she heard, 'Pizza delivery!'

Catrina Edwards (10)

St Joseph's Catholic Primary School, Haywards Heath

HALLOWEEN SURPRISE!

A few weeks ago I was walking down my quiet, eerie road, when suddenly ... I heard a howling sound! At that moment, a very scary ghost leaped out of a bush. However, a bag of shiny sweets spilled out. As it turned out, it was only Halloween!

Helena Booth (10)

St Joseph's Catholic Primary School, Haywards Heath

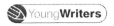

SNOWBALL FIGHT!

Carefully, I chucked a snowball at Charlie! Bending down, Charlie grabbed some snow! I expected to feel the white stuff drip down my back. Nothing! 'Charlie, are you OK?' I questioned. Suddenly, a dark figure turned round, red eyes, no shadow ... 'Argh!'
Then I woke up! 'Mum, what's for breakfast?'

Alice Kelly (10)
St Joseph's Catholic Primary School, Haywards Heath

THE CREEPY HOUSE

It was a dark and scary house and I heard footsteps. I wandered around the old creepy house. There was a door that said: 'Do not enter or you will die!' I stepped back, took a deep breath and opened the door. I switched the light on ...
'Happy birthday!'

Oliver Henry (11)
St Joseph's Catholic Primary School, Haywards Heath

UNTITLED

Silently John rapped on the door to Toadstool Temple, said to be haunted ... It opened with an eerie creak. He moved on through the corridors, weaving in and out of once magnificent suits of armour. Suddenly, he heard an eerie shriek ...
'Surprise!' called his friends. They were the ghosts!

Sean Crawford (10)
St Joseph's Catholic Primary School, Haywards Heath

A SLEEPLESS NIGHT

I couldn't sleep, I was tossing and turning. I was so tired. I decided to turn my lamp on and read, then I saw something move. It was tall, red, white, plump. I thought it was a monster. I heard it say, 'Ho, ho, ho, merry Christmas everyone!'
'Santa!'

Katie Sage (9)
St Joseph's Catholic Primary School, Haywards Heath

RIDDLE SCHOOL

'What? Where am I? What the? What's this?' The boy looks left and picks up an alien coin. 'This could help me get the screws off the vent. Wee! Woo! Uh-oh ...'

Joshua Mongardini (8)

St Joseph's Catholic Primary School, Haywards Heath

SANTA'S TURN ON THE CUBE

Rudolph said, 'Well then step into the cube, let's play. You have to walk along the pole without falling off. You have nine lives, OK.'

'OK.' Santa steps on the pole and uses all his nine lives up and fails.

'Goodbye Santa,' said Rudolph.

Connor William Silvey (8)

St Joseph's Catholic Primary School, Haywards Heath

NO MORE HALLOWEEN

'Trick or treat?' said Simon.
'No, no, no. I don't want to trick you or you would be a fool,' said Miss Ruby to Simon.
'Then how would I get sweets?' said Simon.
'You can make them,' said Miss Ruby.
'But how?' said Simon, sadly crying outside.

Austin Kingsley (8)

St Joseph's Catholic Primary School, Haywards Heath

SANTA'S TRICK

It was Christmas night and Santa Claus turned evil ... When Santa came to my house he wasn't wearing the happy red and white Santa outfit he usually wears. Instead he wore black all over! It turned out it was my little brother tricking me!

Eleanor Rogers (8)

St Joseph's Catholic Primary School, Haywards Heath

THE MONKEY CRASHED OPEN THE DOOR

Suddenly a monkey crashed open the door. 'Argh!' I screamed. 'Help! Help!' I was relieved. It was just my friend in a costume!

Jade Hutchings (8)
St Joseph's Catholic Primary School, Haywards Heath

SEB THE HAMSTER

Sebastian, the brown hamster was in his wheel. A boy came to buy him.
That day the boy played with him. Sebastian bit the boy and saw something red. Sebastian thought he was bleeding but it was just red paint!

Sebastian Norris (9)
St Joseph's Catholic Primary School, Haywards Heath

DON'T BE SILLY

Alicia the egg was home alone, her mum had told her not to climb the wall. Cheeky Alicia did it anyway! She crept along and sat down cautiously. Then she fell off! Lots of farmers came and stuck Alicia together.
When Alicia went home her mum sent her to bed!

Maria Bilton (8)
St Joseph's Catholic Primary School, Haywards Heath

MY BIRTHDAY

Today it's my birthday and I got some really cool presents. I got a safe and some toys. I put them in the safe to keep them safe.
In the night, I heard some funny noises downstairs. I looked and found my toys were out, raiding the kitchen.

Alice McDonald (9)
St Joseph's Catholic Primary School, Haywards Heath

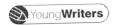

KAYLEY'S SECRET ADVENTURE!

'Help, I'm stuck!' shouted Father Christmas, trying to get down the chimney. Suddenly he fell and landed with a bang. 'Ow!' Santa said. He looked up and to his surprise he saw a girl called Kayley.
She said, 'Wow, it's Father Christmas!' But she was so tired, she fell asleep.

Eleanor Kerr (9)

St Joseph's Catholic Primary School, Haywards Heath

HAPPY BIRTHDAY HONEY

Honey went to the woods because she was finding her friends. She thought her friends had forgotten about her birthday. When she came back home everyone said, 'Happy birthday!'

Laura Craigen (8)

St Joseph's Catholic Primary School, Haywards Heath

THE BUTTON

I had just hit my head. I shouted to my mum but she didn't come. I went up but all I saw were skeletons. Then I saw a bug, I got my bat and hit it. After that I went outside in a machine and pressed a button ...

Logan Crow (8)

St Joseph's Catholic Primary School, Haywards Heath

THE COWBOY THAT NEARLY CAME ALIVE ON CHRISTMAS DAY

It was the night before Christmas when I heard a loud bang and another and another. I got out of bed, I saw tiny footprints. Then I saw a cowboy with a shiny gun. He fired until I woke up. I must have been dreaming.

Louis Chasteauneuf (9)

St Joseph's Catholic Primary School, Haywards Heath

THE RISE OF EXCALIBUR

There was a sword called Excalibur. Excalibur can fly and he went to a creaky old house. A girl called Katie lived there. Katie followed Excalibur to Camelot. On the way, a golden eagle came to kill poor Katie. Excalibur fought back! Excalibur won! Katie fell of a cliff, dead!

Amira Bautista (9)
St Joseph's Catholic Primary School, Haywards Heath

JUGUSLEM'S TORCH

It was an Italian day when the Romans saw a strange glowing button come. Every Roman turned into an animal as a wicked witch came. Only one bear turned the Juguslem Torch. History was seen by one bear.

Matthew Moyo (8)
St Joseph's Catholic Primary School, Haywards Heath

THE RACE

One day I was walking in the park when a snail came. It was the snail that I saw yesterday. He asked, 'Do you want a race?'
I said, 'Yes!'
After the race I said, 'Damn, I lost again!'

Sebastien Hope (8)
St Joseph's Catholic Primary School, Haywards Heath

MONGREL IN THE MOONLIGHT

I was on the picturesque moors during a cold and dark night. There was a steep slope. I slipped and fell! I was in agony. Suddenly, a pink mongrel appeared. It licked my hand while I stroked the ragged thing. I could feel the pain whirring away. I was saved!

Agnes Friend (10)
Soho Parish School, London

UNTITLED

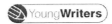

On the 19th of October 1998, Zack Johnson's grandad told him that there was a mysterious criminal haunting the streets of London and his name was Flapjack Dodger. Zack's grandad calculated that he would strike at dawn. He came out at night and stuffed flapjacks into people's faces.

Elliot Elimasi (10)

Soho Parish School, London

THE KNIGHT

The knight was walking down the road when he saw a haunted-looking house surrounded by trees. The overlapping grass swished from side to side. He walked into the house, put the light on, he made a cup of tea and took his costume off from the dress-up party.

Misian Malijoku (11)

Soho Parish School, London

TIGER!

I heard from my friends that there was a monster in a forest, so I set out to the forest.
As soon as I reached the place, I heard snarling, it was a tiger! The tiger struck but I got my penknife and scared it away. Don't mess with tigers!

Shing-Hei To (10)

Soho Parish School, London

FALLING

She screamed as she fell from the toppling skyscraper. After her came the mouse and his trusted steed, the frog with wings. The mouse waving his lasso above him then throwing it, caught her, just as she was to smash into the concrete. Standing again she thanked her hero.

Geo Annabella Sato Rain (11)

Soho Parish School, London

THE MYSTERY HERO!

Katy was walking back home until she fell. Then a man with a green cape ran and dragged her up. 'Thank you but who are you?' said Katy.
'I'm the mystery hero. I have to keep my identity safe!' replied the mystery hero. He left and never ever came back.

Leanne Chan (10)
Soho Parish School, London

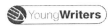

ANNE'S DREAM

All of a sudden, Anne was in a mystical moor. It was damp and dirty. She heard something move in the bushes. She crept up and saw a hooded figure appear. He gave her a key. She found out it was a dream. She opened her hand. It was real.

Inayah Inam (10)
Someries Junior School, Luton

THE GRINCH WHO DIDN'T LIKE CHRISTMAS

There was a town called Newvot, they loved Christmas. The children were celebrating Christmas. They were putting up decorations. The Grinch said, 'I hate Christmas.' He had an idea. He dressed up like Santa and stole the presents! The children had no Christmas!

Kaysha Grant (7)
Someries Junior School, Luton

THE MONSTER IN THE WARDROBE

Once, there lived a little girl and at night she was scared because she thought that there was a big, fluffy monster in her wardrobe.
The next night, she heard a roaring sound and then after that night the big, fluffy monster was never heard of again!

Teya Blakey (8)
Someries Junior School, Luton

WHEN I WENT TO MY COUSIN'S HOUSE

When my cousin, Ransen, opened the door, a jack-in-the-box popped out like a magician and it scared and frightened me. Then we all laughed our heads off. We all had the greatest time ever.
We can't wait to go back and visit them again.

Minuka Wanigatunge (7)
Someries Junior School, Luton

GOLDILOCKS

One day a little girl called Goldilocks was walking through the woods. Looking around she saw a little house. In the house she saw three bowls of porridge and ate the littlest bowl. Then she tried the chairs and broke the little one. So she went to bed.

Shehani Enderage Dona
Someries Junior School, Luton

A TRIP TO THE BEACH

One morning I was packing to go to the beach. I was really excited because my family were coming. When we got there I got my bucket and spade and made a wonderful sandcastle.
At the end of a lovely day we went home.

Isabella Pearson

Someries Junior School, Luton

SCHOOL DAY

When I woke up, I realised I was late for school. Yikes! I rushed to the bathroom, had a shower then had breakfast. I brushed my teeth then got dressed.
We hurried to school like Lewis Hamilton. We got to school and I strolled into class, late but dry.

Luke Parkes (7)

Someries Junior School, Luton

GOLDILOCKS

Goldilocks was walking in the woods when she saw a house. She went inside and saw three chairs. Then she saw three bowls of porridge. She ate the smallest bowl. She went upstairs and fell asleep on the smallest bed. Then the bears came home and she ran away!

Patryk Krzywonos (8)
Someries Junior School, Luton

YEAR 4'S CHRISTMAS PLAY

Yesterday afternoon me and my class went to see Year 4's Christmas play. During their Christmas play we had to join in some words on one of the parts. Father Christmas had to come on with no trainers! It was very exciting to watch. The show was good.

Chloe Secker
Someries Junior School, Luton

A SCHOOL DAY

It was school and I was very excited because it was our school trip today. 3S and 3W's trip. We were going to Stockwood Park for the day.
After we did some work then we had some playtime. Me and Shannay played a game, then we got our coats.

Emily Loft (7)

Someries Junior School, Luton

STAR WARS

Yoda and Luke Skywalker were hiding behind a big rock. Suddenly, they heard a noise, it was coming in front. Yoda put his head out and saw the captain. The captain was called General Grievous. Yoda and Luke Skywalker made a plan. Yoda called Chewbacca to come in his spaceship.

Ethan O'Dell (7)

Someries Junior School, Luton

THE MAGICAL BUNNY

Once upon a time, there was a child called Lucy. She had a white pet bunny called Holly.
One day, when she was feeding him, he came out. She looked outside and it was snowing. She rushed outside to play in the snow.

Amy Jarvis (8)

Someries Junior School, Luton

VIETNAM AT WAR

The battle was coming! Vietnam was at war. I ran to find shelter. I had nothing. Bombs were exploding around me. Guns were being fired. I was in danger! No one could save me now. I was face to face with a gun. I was glad to go.

Mollie-Mae Fisher (10)

Someries Junior School, Luton

THE CHRISTMAS BEAST

Up in the mountains lived a beast who loved Christmas but he tried to be nice but it didn't work. While he was asleep a little girl climbed up the mountains and put a candy cane in his stocking. Suddenly he woke up, 'Thank you,' she shouted and smiled.

James Lewis (9)

Someries Junior School, Luton

THE ISLAND OF THE LOST SOULS

Daniel was strolling home from a hard day at school. He felt weird. Seconds later his soul got taken.
A myth says that they get to an island and stay in it for nine days. Daniel's parents were shocked to hear this.

Ronak Gandhi (10)

Someries Junior School, Luton

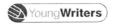

IT WAS ONLY A CAT

The night was getting darker. Theo was getting very scared. Him and his family went camping for the night. *Crash! Bang!* Something was happening. Theo was petrified. He wanted to run home. They were only in his garden. The sound came again. He bravely opened the door … 'A cat!' he cried.

Rakeem Kamara (10)

Someries Junior School, Luton

THE DARK MORNING

As Tom woke up he shouted, 'Morning!' But weirdly, no one replied. He tiptoed down the stairs. The lights turned on, he sat on the sofa.
'Boo!' yelled his mum.
Tom got a fright. Tears dropped from his eyes. His mum laughed. The door opened, it was his dad.

Nico Brown (9)

Someries Junior School, Luton

LITTLE RED RIDING HOOD

Little Red Riding Hood went to see her grandma. When she got there they sat at the table drinking milk. Suddenly, a wolf burst through the door, threatening to eat them. Grandma got up and started doing karate kicks at him. The wolf was beaten up by Grandma.

Holly Douglas (9)

Someries Junior School, Luton

A DAY IN FRANCE

His family were going to the biggest building in the whole of France. They took their cat Poppy. He was scared of heights. Poppy stayed far back. They just arrived at the top of the building. Poppy jumped out of the elevator first, before anyone else could.

Shannon Mullen (9)

Someries Junior School, Luton

THE GREAT MUMMY SEARCH

Callum and Josh went to fight the mummy. Callum and Josh were searching the pyramid. Then Callum and Josh stepped in a trap. A giant chocolate ball attacked Callum and Josh. Behind them they saw a tomb. Josh opened the tomb. Then a mummy came out ...

Callum Brady (9)

Someries Junior School, Luton

THE FREAKY MAN

Jennifer was walking home from school when she tripped on the ice and sliced her leg. When she tried to get up slowly, an old, ghostly, freaky man jumped in front of her and she jumped back and screamed. She ran back to her house and locked the front door.

Melissa Rylands (9)

Someries Junior School, Luton

THE CREEPY HOUSE

Sam was walking home but when he got there it was dark and deserted. He heard a plate smash in the kitchen. He felt very uneasy. Sam felt something scratching his feet. He ran to the light switch but when he turned the light on, it was only his cat.

Dean Kemp (9)

Someries Junior School, Luton

THE CROOKED HOUSE

As I arrived home from school I saw an old man walk into the old house across the road. It's been there for years. Something was going on.
'Leave that man alone!' Mum said.
I ignored her and went straight over there, to see him disappearing through the door!

Brooke Turner (9)

Someries Junior School, Luton

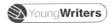

THE SCARY-FACED MAN

Rhys was jogging down the steep hill, when he came across a blacked-out house. He went to look. Suddenly, a spooky face came sprinting out at him. 'Please don't hurt me!'
'I'm OK. Would you please be my friend?'
'I don't know, you're a stranger. Where are your friends?'

Daniel McCool (10)
Someries Junior School, Luton

UNTITLED

The house creaked. A ghost was lurking through the house, looking spookily through the broken window. Daniel was walking towards the house. He tiptoed through the door. Then he saw the ghost and asked him if he was friendly.
The ghost said, 'No!'
'Argh!' Daniel ran for his life.

Joshua Stephens
Someries Junior School, Luton

AS I RAN

As I ran down the hallway I heard a scream; it came from upstairs. I ran outside, I looked to where it came from. I was scared. I ran home. No one was in. I shouted, 'Mum, where are you?' The scream came again and I woke.

James Eddy (10)
Winslow CE Combined School, Winslow

THE DREAM GHOST

She opened her eyes. There in front of her stood a shimmering figure. She blinked. The figure drew closer.
'You think you're dreaming, don't you?'
She started to shiver. The figure was almost touching her. 'No! I don't! Go away!' she wailed.
'You'll go first!' he chuckled.
She was gone.

Elizabeth Burch (10)
Winslow CE Combined School, Winslow

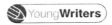

THE LONG WAY HOME

The field of crimson flowers stretched out like a pool of blood. Poppies whispering the reminders of the dead. The soldiers' heavy boots dredged through the field. Sunshine peeked over the horizon, welcoming, beckoning. The soldiers started the long walk home. Back from the war.

Sanna Baur (10)

Winslow CE Combined School, Winslow

BUZZ ...

Tick-tock .... that's the clock. *Flushhh* ... that's the toilet chain. *Thump* ... that's me falling out of bed. *Buzzz* ... what's that? *Buzzz* ... there it is again. Its dark shape looms closer ... Shadows are all over the wall. I turn my head around to see ... a bee flying out of the window!

Alexadra Julier (10)

Winslow CE Combined School, Winslow

THE THING

Ben got home from school. He was sure his dad was meant to be home.
He went to the kitchen, with its cold, cracked tiles. Not there. So he went down to the cellar. There were cobwebs in his pale, white face. Then he saw it ... !

George Edwards (11)
Winslow CE Combined School, Winslow

SHOT DEAD

The bullet whizzed away a second before the shot. Five more followed. A sharp pain hit me. I looked down to see blood pouring out of me. A black cloaked figure emerged. Out came a needle from his cloak. It went into me. All went black.

Thomas Stacey (10)
Winslow CE Combined School, Winslow

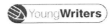

THE NIGHTMARE

As I travelled through space and time, I heard a voice squeaking, 'I'm a princess!'
Shortly after, it exploded.
I woke up. My forehead was sweating. I soon noticed it was just a dream and drifted back to sleep.

Ben Glass (11)

Winslow CE Combined School, Winslow

MUMMY?

I heard an ear-splitting scream! I turned around; I looked around; I screamed! There was my mum with no make-up on! 'Who woke me up?'

Rivkah D'Amon (10)

Winslow CE Combined School, Winslow

THE WALL

'Yum!' gobbled the wall. 'I love humans.' It was a sunny day in Toadstool Temple. Everyone was enjoying the market apart from one thing, Rumpety-Dumpety. Rumpety-Dumpety was an unusual wall, he ate humans!
One day, when everyone was walking past ...
'Argh!'
A family had been eaten whole.

Mollie Burns (10)

Winslow CE Combined School, Winslow

DARK WOODS

In the dark woods was a little house. Nothing was in the house and there was no one about. Then there was a wolf and I ran and locked the door. The wolf tried and tried to get in and kill me and then the wolf smashed in and roared.

Edward Penfold (10)

Winslow CE Combined School, Winslow

NOISES

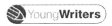

It was dark as I was walking home. Owls were hooting and the wind was screaming. I stepped in the house, floorboards creaked then suddenly, a monster with blood-dripping fangs emerged. I thundered upstairs and hid in my bed.

Nathan Veal (11)
Winslow CE Combined School, Winslow

DARKNESS

In the distance, I noticed a shadowy house. I walked towards it. I trudged into the house cautiously, looked both ways and decided it was safe. Suddenly, I tripped and started falling. The air was diagnosed with dust. Then I stopped falling, my eyes closed. I saw darkness. Just darkness.

Ryan Clark (11)
Winslow CE Combined School, Winslow

MONSTERS

It was a dark and stormy night when, out of Pixie Palace, was a dark, evil monster. It was like smoke and it was made out of fire ashes. Who would save Pixie Palace?

Ella Abery

Winslow CE Combined School, Winslow

THE MUTATION

John was an ordinary boy who went to school like everybody else does.
One day, John got bitten by a venomous viper. 'Ouch!' screamed John. 'What was that?'
'It was me,' hissed the viper.
'What's going to happen to me?'
He became a venomous viper.

Emily Hunt (11)

Winslow CE Combined School, Winslow

THE CRUMBLY BUILDING

I stood outside an old, crumbly building. I daren't take a step in. But I did. Shrieks were coming out of nowhere. I shouted to them, but the shrieks just got louder every step. Suddenly, a hand touched my shoulder and dragged me away from the building.

Joshua Cull (10)

Winslow CE Combined School, Winslow

THE BLOOD-RED TRUCK

On a Saturday night there was a red van which drove in complete darkness. One night they snatched a dog, they heard a laugh and a bang, the dog vanished and a face appeared in the mirror. The men were never to be seen again.

Emily Horne (10)

Winslow CE Combined School, Winslow

MURDER

When Grace was entering her house no one seemed to be in. She thought that her mum and dad were meant to be in but she didn't care.
She saw a glimpse of a bright light coming from upstairs. She went upstairs and it was ... a murderer!

Danielle Crossley (10)

Winslow CE Combined School, Winslow

DARK

A cold shiver vibrated down his spine. It was dark and deserted, but in the gloom, he didn't feel alone. He scrambled about for a light of some sort, but instead cold drained fingers gripped his sweaty palm. Another covered his mouth, muffling his scream and drawing him slowly backwards.

Skyla Baily (10)

Winslow CE Combined School, Winslow

MIDNIGHT

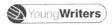

It was midnight. The once formidable castle was now in ruins, lying before him. As he walked closer he could hear voices, cruel, raspy voices. He kept on walking, he could not stop himself, then he panicked; something he would later regret. Then someone walked out, 'Die!' and silence. Nothing.

Sam Ray-Chaudhuri (10)
Winslow CE Combined School, Winslow

THE MIDNIGHT SURPRISE

It was midnight. Melissa couldn't sleep. She heard shrieking murmurs. Her parents were dead; she lived in an abandoned castle, all alone. A shadow suddenly cast over her fragile bed. Melissa sunk into the ragged duvet. *It's getting closer,* she thought, *it's a nightmare.* Suddenly her pet mouse scrambled in.

Madeleine Thomas (10)
Winslow CE Combined School, Winslow

CHICKEN WANTS TO KNOW THE TIME

One day a chicken wanted to know the time and the fox said, 'Come to my house.'
When they got there Mr Fox closed the curtains and when the clock struck six he said, 'Dinner time!'
The chicken opened his mouth and ate the fox all up.
'No regrets!'

Benjamin Wilder (10)
Winslow CE Combined School, Winslow

A DAY IN THE LIFE OF CHERYL COLE

As she stepped into the fancy limo, her make-up artist was smothering her with gorgeous make-up ready for her TV appearance. She had to perform her latest ever single in front of all her screaming fans.
She was glad to get it all over and done with.

Lucy Ray-Chaudhuri (10)
Winslow CE Combined School, Winslow

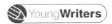

HOUSE OF HORROR

I walked downstairs, I heard a creak on the floor. I ran into the kitchen and 'it' followed me. I got frightened, more than frightened. Every step I took, I could hear a creak. I turned, no one there. I stood laughing because I found out it was me.

Georgia Attwell (11)
Winslow CE Combined School, Winslow

BEACH OF MONKEYS

I could feel a cold breeze on my fingers. I stood up and these monkeys were staring at me. I was on an island. A monkey shouted, 'The king of fire's here!'
They took me to a cave, they were singing 'Ring of Fire'. They threw me off a cliff!

Orla Parry (11)
Winslow CE Combined School, Winslow

PIXIE PATH - GHOSTLY GOINGS-ON

It was strange that morning when Phoebe, the pixie, woke up. There was a cold breeze. The window was locked before she went to bed.
She heard five knocks at her door. She hid behind the bed. The door slowly opened ...
'Surprise!' her parents shouted as Phoebe screamed for help!

Olivia Adams (10)
Winslow CE Combined School, Winslow

THE WIDE-MOUTHED FROG!

There was once a wide-mouthed frog. He met a giraffe.
'Who are you?'
'I'm a giraffe. Who are you?'
'A wide-mouthed frog. Bye.'
Then he met a lion. 'Who are you?'
'I'm a lion and I eat wide-mouthed frogs!'
'Well, you don't see many around, do you?'

Amie Birch (10)
Winslow CE Combined School, Winslow

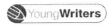

GHOSTLY GOINGS-ON

One dark, stormy night, Sven was watching '28 Days Later', alone. He heard a smash. 'Damn kids,' he whispered. The weather was meek. He paused the film. Silence was surrounding the room. The lights flickered. 'OK, this is weird!'
'Surprise!' said a voice.
'Oh, Mum!'

Harry Winchester (10)

Winslow CE Combined School, Winslow

THE MAN

I crept up to the horrible, fragile door. I knocked. Silence was upon me. The shattered door opened with a creak, *creak!* There, standing before me, was a man dressed in deathly clothes. 'What do you want?' he said, with blood dripping down from his mouth.
'Argh!' I ran.

Ellie Thomas (10)

Winslow CE Combined School, Winslow

HUMPTY-DUMPTY HAD A GREAT FALL

It was a dark, stormy night; nobody was in sight. Humpty-Dumpty stood on the wall. He looked around and without a breath, bent his knees and … jumped. The next day, a little girl came skipping past the wall. Suddenly, she screamed: Humpty-Dumpty had had a great fall. Dead!

Jessica Wright (11)

Winslow CE Combined School, Winslow

LOST IN THE WOODS

They were alone in the woods lost, no one but themselves and the midnight moon. A pack of wolves nearby howled at the silky white moon. They were lost, lost in the woods alone …

Cerys Allen (10)

Winslow CE Combined School, Winslow

BLACK AS BLACK

Darkness shadowed the road ahead. I followed the shadows of the moon's light. Down the winding path I travelled on and on. The darker it got, the colder I got.
The shadows stopped, silence fell ...
'Boo!'
A mouse! I jumped. I fled. 'Argh!'

Matthew Taylor (10)
Winslow CE Combined School, Winslow

YOUNG WRITERS INFORMATION

We hope you have enjoyed reading this book - and that you will continue to enjoy it in the coming years.
If you like reading and creative writing drop us a line, or give us a call, and we'll send you a free information pack.

Alternatively if you would like to order further copies of this book or any of our other titles, then please give us a call or log onto our website at **www.youngwriters.co.uk**

Young Writers Information
Remus House
Coltsfoot Drive
Peterborough
PE2 9BF
Tel: (01733) 890066